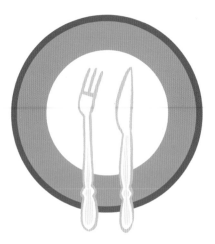

To Matthew, my well-mannered
little man, with love – S.M.

the witch & the dog

A LESSON IN MANNERS

Story by Sue McMillan

Illustrations by Owen Davey

 OOD manners don't cost a penny, but they do help people get along. For most of us they are easy to learn. But for some, a helping hand is needed ...

• • • • • • • • •

DAPHNE is an enchanting witch. Thanks to her politeness and excellent manners she is often asked to work her magic, taming tearaways, transforming troublesome teens and making awful animals into the perfect pets.

She takes on any challenge, even Harry, a dog who arrived with no manners at all ...

WHEN there was a knock on the door, Daphne didn't know that there was a bundle of trouble outside. If she had, she might not have opened it. But she did, and found a scruffy mongrel with chocolate-coloured eyes and a cheeky expression that seemed to say, 'Watch out! I'm a pickle!'

She read the note that came with him:

Dearest Daphne,

We are desperate and just can't cope with Harry. Please give him a loving home. p.s. You will have to teach him some manners. Good luck!

"OW do you do?" she asked politely, holding out her right hand for Harry to shake.

When you meet someone for the first time, shake their right hand and say, 'How do you do?' or 'Hello'.

UT Harry leapt out of his basket and smothered Daphne with wet, slobbery kisses.

As a rule, kissing should be kept for family and close friends.

DAPHNE tried not to notice Harry's blunders, but the rest of the day passed in a series of doggy disasters that were hard to ignore. Harry ...

... knocked over a visitor ...

Ouch!

... gobbled his food greedily ...

... burped loudly without saying excuse me ...

Belch!

... and, worst of all, left a doggy
poo on Daphne's best rug.

Daphne had had enough.

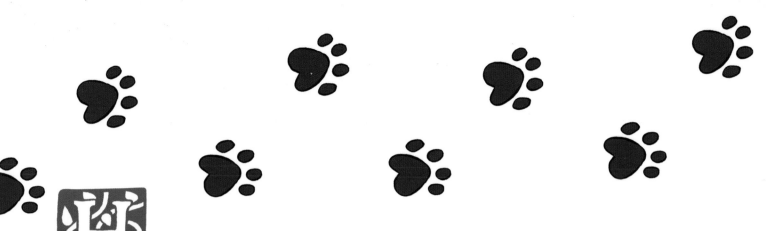

HARRY felt ashamed. Daphne was right. He didn't have any friends. Were his horrible habits and rudeness to blame? "Can ya teach me some of them manners things?" he muttered.

Daphne picked up her *Magical Manners* book and nodded. "Yes, I believe I can. But you will have to work very hard!" she warned. "And if you don't, I'll turn you into a toad! We'll start again with a proper how do you do."

Daphne was pleased that Harry offered his paw, less so when she realised it was muddy. But it was a start at least.

Pass the
soap

UTTING on her specs, Daphne examined Harry more closely. His appearance left a lot to be desired. "Oh dear!" she sniffed. "We will have to start from scratch and get rid of those awful fleas!"

Bathing made Harry grouchy, but Daphne was firm. No more messy mutt! If Harry was to stay, he had to be a polished pooch.

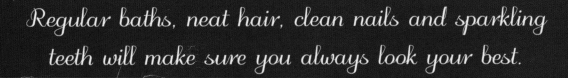

Regular baths, neat hair, clean nails and sparkling teeth will make sure you always look your best.

THAT evening, Daphne showed Harry to the table. He was looking smarter. She hoped she could polish his table manners to match. Sadly, she found that when it came to cutlery, Harry would need a lot of help.

There is more to dining than food. Sit up straight in your chair. Be relaxed and keep your elbows off the table. Place your napkin on your lap, not around your neck.

Wait until everyone is ready to begin. Don't play
with your cutlery. If there's more than one set of cutlery,
begin with the ones furthest from your plate.

DAPHNE chewed her food politely. Harry munched open-mouthed, licking his lips and smacking his chops. His supper splattered everywhere as he loudly burped and barked. Daphne lost her appetite.

If you need something, ask someone to pass it to you. Don't forget to say please and thank you!

WHEN it came to spinach, Harry cringed. "Yuck!" he cried as he sniffed it suspiciously. "It smells horrid and it's all slimy!"

Daphne frowned. "Toads are slimier, Harry," she warned. Harry didn't fancy being turned into pond life, so he gave the spinach a cautious lick.

If there is something on your plate that you don't like, don't make a fuss. Do your best to be polite.

 FTER dessert, Harry spat his peach stone across the table, then bounded from his chair with another ground-shaking burp.

Daphne took out her spell book and opened it at 'Toads'. Harry panicked. "Fanks for dinner. 'Cept the spinach – that was 'orrible!" he said, flashing her his best smile.

Daphne supposed it would do for now. Teaching a dog new tricks would take time.

To show you have finished your meal, put your cutlery together on your plate. Wait for everyone to do the same. Then ask to leave the table. Don't forget to say thank you!

RADUALLY, day-by-day, Harry grew well-mannered and groomed. Daphne decided the time had come to reward him with a gift.

When you receive a gift, don't forget to say thank you.
It is most polite to write a thoughtful note ...

HEN Harry handed her a thank you note, Daphne was very happy. Even though the tone wasn't quite what she'd had in mind:

Dear Daphne,
It was very kind of you to give me a monocle and a bow tie, but they're not really my cup of tea. Any chance you could change them for a bone?
Harry xxx

... even if the present isn't quite to your taste.

 APHNE tried her best to teach Harry to share. Harry tried his best. Most of the time ...

When it came to food, he often forgot. It was very hard to share Daphne's delicious cakes. They were just too tasty.

Whether it's playtime, mealtime or snack-time, learning to share is important.

Parp!

Never help yourself without offering to others first.

ARRY and Daphne often played games. Harry loved pick-up-sticks but Daphne wasn't so keen. Harry forgot to take turns and picked up all the sticks himself.

When playing sports or games, remember to take turns.

APHNE liked playing cards, even though Harry always won. Then Daphne found out that he was cheating.

They also played chess. "A gentleman is gracious when he loses", Daphne told Harry. But when she beat him at chess, Harry was cross. He ran off with the board and buried it in the garden.

Never cheat and don't be a sore loser.

Smile, be gracious and say, "Well played!" to the winner.

VEN so, Daphne didn't give up. Harry would be a pet she could be proud of, with manners to match her own.

Good manners take time to learn, but they
will give you the confidence to handle any occasion.

After all, good manners can take you anywhere ...

HARRY was now a polished pooch and felt Daphne deserved a present for tackling his horrible habits. He carefully chose her a gift he knew she would really love ... a cat.

"How perfect!" Daphne bubbled, giving Harry a heart-felt hug.

"She looks well-bred," she said, stroking the cat's delicate head. "Let's call her Grace. Grace by name, Grace by nature ..."

To thank a friend, a thoughtful note
or well-chosen gift is a good idea.

HE cat looked up at Daphne with her deep, emerald eyes and yawned. Then she burped and picked her nose. Cackling, she trumped and a terrible smell filled the room.

"Pooh! How rude!" cried Harry and Daphne together.

Daphne was dejected. Harry was horrified.

**H**ARRY handed Daphne her *Magical Manners* book. Turning to each other they both said,

We'll have to start from scratch ...

Golly gosh

First published in Great Britain in 2012 by
Far Far Away Books and Media, Ltd.
20-22 Bedford Row, London, WC1 R4JS

ISBN: 978-1-908786-03-6 (hardback)
ISBN: 978-1-908786-63-0 (paperback)

A CIP catalogue record for this book is available from the British Library

Printed and bound in Portugal by Printer Portuguesa

FSC
www.fsc.org
MIX
Paper from
responsible sources
FSC® C006423

All Far Far Away books can be ordered from www.centralbooks.com

www.farfarawaybooks.com